JOSEPHINA
HATES HER NAME

DIANA ENGEL

Morrow Junior Books
New York

For my mother
and for Nonna

Copyright © 1989 by Diana Engel
Inquiries should be addressed to
William Morrow and Company, Inc.,
105 Madison Avenue,
New York, NY 10016.

Printed in Hong Kong.
1   2   3   4   5   6   7   8   9   10

Library of Congress Cataloging-in-Publication Data
Engel, Diana.
Josephina hates her name / Diana Engel.
p.   cm.
Summary: After Grandma explains that she named Josephina after Grandma's
talented, daring older sister, Josephina starts to appreciate her
unusual name.
ISBN 0-688-07795-1.   ISBN 0-688-07796-X (lib. bdg.)
[1. Names, Personal—Fiction.   2. Great-aunts—Fiction.]
I. Title.
PZ7.E69874Jm   1989
88-1500   CIP   AC   [E]—dc19

On a wet and gloomy Saturday, Josephina played with her friends Amy and Sarah in her bedroom at the top of the stairs.

"Let's trade names," said Josephina, looking at herself in the mirror.

"Okay," said Amy. "I'll be Sarah."

"And I'll be Amy," said Sarah.

"But what about me?" cried Josephina. "Doesn't anyone want my name?"

"Well," said Amy, "it's so . . . unusual."

"You can pick another name," suggested Sarah, "any name you want."

"All right," said Josephina, feeling better, "I'll be Jenny-Michelle."

But after her friends had gone, Josephina sat alone in her
room. She looked at her collecting bag, waiting to be filled.
Josephina was a great collector. She loved gathering anything
and everything from the world outside. But today she felt
empty, like the bag, and angry as well.

My name is *ugly*, she thought. It's old-fashioned and unusual.

"J-O-S-E-P-H-I-N-A," she said slowly.

All she could picture was a clumsy old cow climbing over a fence.

It's all my parents' fault for giving me such a terrible name, she thought.

That night, Josephina sat with Grandma, pinching the ends
off a pile of string beans.

"Why did my parents name me Josephina?" she asked.

"Because I wanted them to," said Grandma.

"*You* named me Josephina?"

"I had a feeling that you'd be special," said Grandma, "so I gave you a special name."

"But why *Josephina*?"

"It was my sister's name," said Grandma.

"Your sister probably hated her name, too!"

Beans went flying in every direction.

After dinner Rose tried to cheer up her younger sister.
"I saw some boxes down the street, full of stuff you'd really like," she said. "If we get out early tomorrow, we can beat the garbage collectors!"

"Of course *you're* happy," said Josephina to Rose. "You have a pretty name. It even smells nice!"

She stormed from the room, stomped up the stairs, and slammed the bedroom door.

Much later, Josephina heard a knock. Grandma peeked in.
"Let me tell you about your great-aunt," Grandma said.

Slowly, the story began. Her words wrapped around
Josephina like one of the warm and cozy sweaters she was
always knitting.

"We lived in a place far, far from here, across a wide ocean," said Grandma. "It was hot and green and very beautiful."

"My sister Josephina was beautiful, too. And very brave.
"Every day she went deep into the woods with sketchbooks
and pencils, looking for birds and bugs and flowers. She
drew them all and brought home anything and everything."

"There was no one else like her in our family and no one like her in our town.

"I followed her everywhere. I saw such wonderful things—"

"—and some things that were not so wonderful."

"At night my sister would whisper to me in the dark,
'Someday we'll go to the Great Jungle. We'll see giant
butterflies and snakes the color of emeralds!' "

"One morning, when we were nearly grown up, Josephina
came to me, dressed in traveling clothes.

" 'Let's go,' she said. 'The time has come to see the Great
Jungle!'

"My face must have shown that I was full of fear."

"Josephina kissed me. She placed something in my hand and was gone."

"It was her gold locket. Inside were a picture of Josephina and a few strands of her hair."

"Sometime later, a young man came to our town. When I was with him, I felt full of happiness. He asked me to marry him and sail far, far away to his home across the ocean."

"Was I brave enough to go?
"Touching my sister's locket, I heard my voice say, Yes."

"As I sailed with your grandfather on seas as black as ink, I
felt brave and full and as big as the night sky."

Josephina blinked.

"Where is your sister now, Grandma?" she asked.

"Living in the Great Jungle," said Grandma, "and she would want you to have this."

Josephina felt something in her hand. Grandma was gone.
She lay on the bed, holding her great-aunt's locket. Soon
she slept and dreamed the most wonderful dream.

Josephina, Grandma, and her great-aunt flew across the sky, smelling the nighttime flowers and touching the treetops with their toes.

They slept together under leaves as big as tents, while the face of the Great Jungle Moon smiled down on them.

Josephina woke early the next morning. She couldn't wait
to tell her friends about Grandma's story.
They were mighty impressed with Josephina's great-aunt.

"Let's trade names," said Sarah. "I'll be Josephina."
"No," said Amy, "I'll be Josephina."
"No!" said Josephina proudly. "I'll be Josephina!"

And she was.